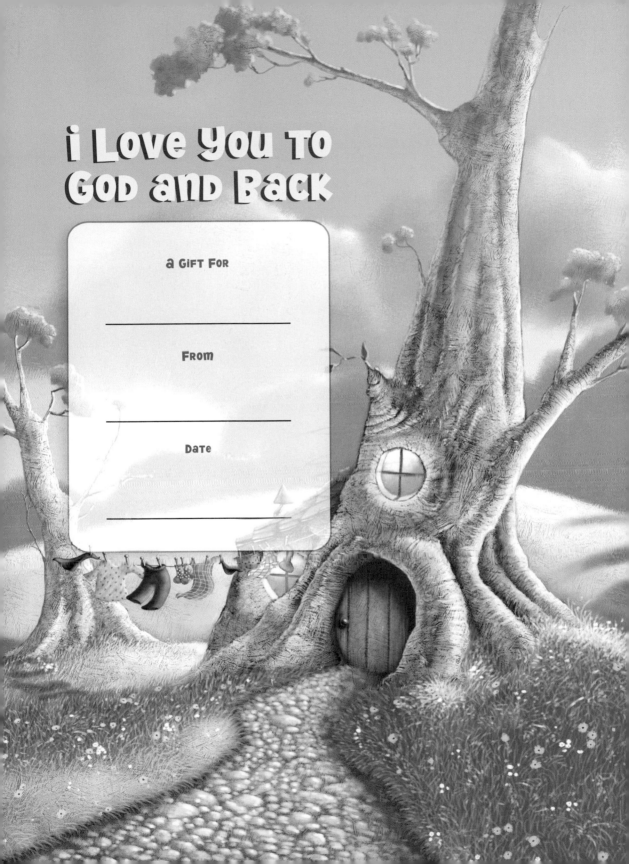

i Love You to God and Back

A GIFT FOR

_____

FROM

_____

DATE

_____

Published in Nashville, Tennessee, by Tommy Nelson. Tommy Nelson is a registered trademark of Thomas Nelson, Inc.

Published in association with Sharlene Martin, Martin Literary Management LLC.

Thomas Nelson, Inc., titles may be purchased in bulk for educational, business, fund-raising, or sales promotional use. For information, please e-mail SpecialMarkets@ThomasNelson.com.

ISBN: 978-1-4003-2082-0

Library of Congress Control Number: 2012945378

Printed in China

13 14 15 16 17 LEO 6 5 4 3 2 1

i Love You to God and Back

Amanda Lamb

Illustrated by Czes Pachela

A Division of Thomas Nelson Publishers

NASHVILLE   DALLAS   MEXICO CITY   RIO DE JANEIRO

**To my own precious little bunnies,
Chloe and Mallory.**

To mama and papa bunnies everywhere,
With all our hustling and hopping here and there, it
takes a concerted effort to stop and focus on the big picture—on
what really matters. Do our little bunnies know that
we love them? Do they know that *God* loves
them? Do they know how to speak to Him,
how to share their secrets and fears? Do
we model that behavior for them?

On the surface, *I Love You to God and Back* is a sweet story about a bunny family that your little bunnies will love. But at the heart level, the story models the habit of spending time with God, and it reassures little ones of a love that never ends. Of all of the life lessons I want to share with my children, these two outshine them all.

My prayer for you is that these little bunnies—along with the habit of seeking God's never-ending love—will find a special place in your homes and in your hearts.

Amanda Lamb

Mommy Bunny cleaned up the last of the carrot-cookie crumbs. "Time for bed!" her voice rang out to her three little bunnies. "Race you!" Bitty Bunny called as she scrambled to put her toys away.

"I LOVE YOU TO THE TOY BOX AND BACK!" Mommy told her bunnies.

"And I love *you* to the toy box and back!" said Bitty Bunny as she dropped her blocks and stuffed bear into the box.

Bitty Bunny began to search for her favorite snuggly pajamas. "Mommy, do you know just how much I love you?" she asked.

"Hmmm. I'm not sure," Mommy said with a smile. "How much *do* you love me?"

"ALL THE WAY TO THE DRESSER AND BACK!" Bitty Bunny replied.

"*Brush, brush, brushy-brush. Wash them really clean,*"
Bitty Bunny sang through a mouthful of bubbles.

"*Bristle, whistle toothbrush. Make your toothbrush
sing,*" Mommy finished.

"Know what, Mommy?" Bitty Bunny began, holding her toothbrush out as far as her little arm could reach. **"i Love you aLL THe way To my TOOTHBRUSH aND BaCK."**

Mommy Bunny smiled. "My, that's a lot of love," she said as she wiped bubbles from Bitty Bunny's chin.

The bunnies all scampered to the bookshelf
to choose their stories.

When it was Bitty Bunny's turn, she searched
the shelves for her favorite book, the one where
Mommy would do all the funny voices.

"i love you to the bed and back!"

Bitty Bunny declared as she raced with her
books to the big, fluffy bed.

Bitty climbed into bed, held her favorite book, and snuggled close. First, Bitty read to Mommy. Just like Mommy, she did the squeaky baby voice. Just like Mommy, she did the really deep daddy voice. And just like Mommy, she read the last page soft and slow. Then Mommy read to Bitty.

"You're the best reader in the whole wide world," Bitty told Mommy when she was finished.

Snuggly jammies on. Teeth sparkling. Favorite story read.
Now Bitty was ready for the best part of bedtime.

"What do we want to say to God tonight?" Mommy asked,
rubbing Bitty's back.

Bitty Bunny closed her eyes and started to pray.

Dear God, thank You for loving me so much. I want You to know how much I love You. I praise You for all You have created for us—for the sunshiny day, the purple flowers by the mailbox, the green grass under my swing, and the three baby birds in the tree by the clothesline. I love You so much, and I'm glad You made this beautiful world!

"GOD LOVES IT WHEN YOU PRAISE HIM," Mommy whispered, kissing Bitty right between her ears.

Bitty Bunny closed her eyes even tighter
for the next part of her prayer.

And God, I'm really sorry for not sharing with Sissy and for scribbling on my brother's coloring page today. I'll try to do what You say and to love them more. Help me to do my best for You.

"GOD LOVES WHEN OUR HEARTS ARE SORRY FOR BEING UNKIND," said Mommy Bunny.

Bitty Bunny wiggled a bit as she thought about Grandma.

God, please help Grandma Bunny feel better. I love her so much, and I know she can't wait to eat cookies and play checkers with me again soon.

Mommy Bunny gave Bitty a little squeeze. **"GOD SMILES WHEN WE CARE ABOUT OTHERS,"** she said.

Bitty Bunny then thought about her very many blessings. How would she fit them all into one prayer?

And, God, thank You for everything You give me every day. Thank You for letting me play outside today. Thank You for the yummy chocolate ice cream this afternoon. And thank You so, so much for a close, loving family that loves me no matter what. In Jesus' name, amen!

Mommy Bunny grinned. "I think that's my favorite part," she said with a wink. **"GOD IS HAPPY WHEN WE LOVE OUR FAMILY."**

Mommy tucked the covers under Bitty's chin. She felt so sleepy, but she didn't want to miss what came next.

Mommy Bunny turned out the light. "Time for sleep," she said. **"i Love you To your Dreams anD BacK, LiTTLe one."**

"I love you more," a sleepy voice replied.

"I love you the most," Mommy whispered into one of Bitty Bunny's floppy ears.

"I love you the mostest!" answered Bitty with a giggle, and then Mommy turned toward the next little bunny's bedroom door.

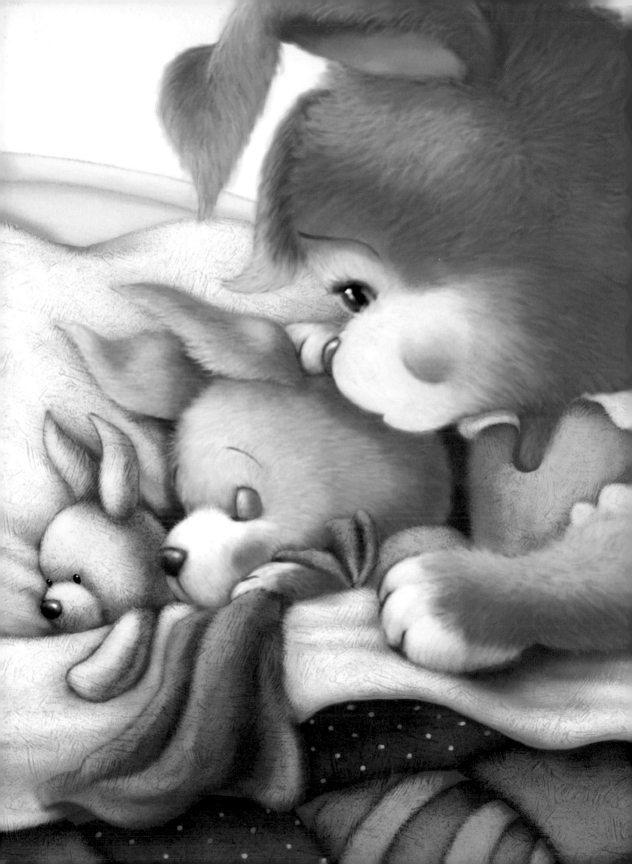

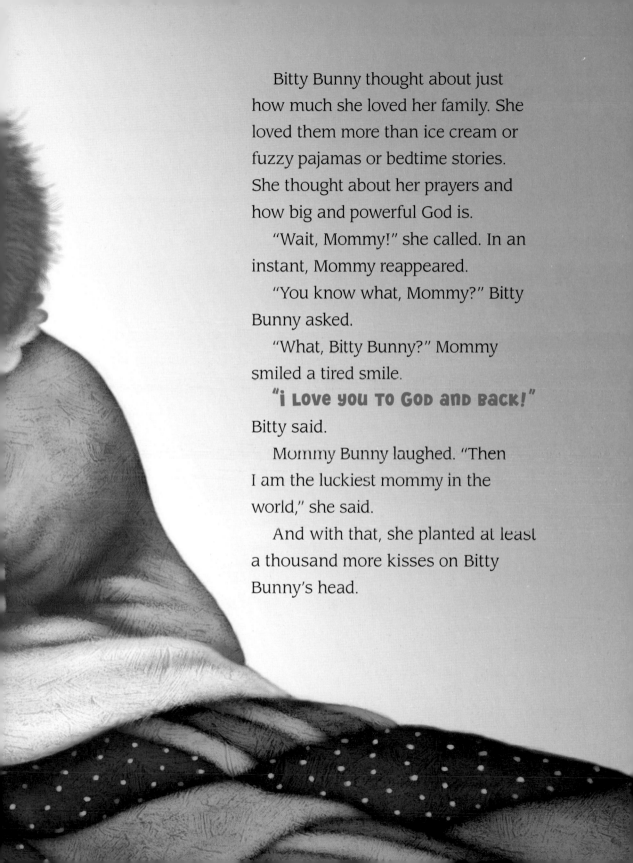

Bitty Bunny thought about just how much she loved her family. She loved them more than ice cream or fuzzy pajamas or bedtime stories. She thought about her prayers and how big and powerful God is.

"Wait, Mommy!" she called. In an instant, Mommy reappeared.

"You know what, Mommy?" Bitty Bunny asked.

"What, Bitty Bunny?" Mommy smiled a tired smile.

"I love you to God and back!" Bitty said.

Mommy Bunny laughed. "Then I am the luckiest mommy in the world," she said.

And with that, she planted at least a thousand more kisses on Bitty Bunny's head.

Bitty Bunny snuggled under the covers, knowing just how much she was loved. Even in the dark, she could feel her mommy's smile.

Love is like that, so big and bright that you always know it's there. And God's love? Through our good days and our bad days—and all the way back again—God's love is the *biggest* love of all.

Dear God,

Will You fill our home and hearts with Your love?
Will you help us, big and small, young and old,
to remember that Your love is always helping us,
healing us, and holding us together in this world?
And most of all, will You help us to show one
another a love as big as Yours?

In Your name, amen.